POLAR BEAR

GOAT

FROG

WHALE

CLAM

HOUND

OWL

GIRAFFE

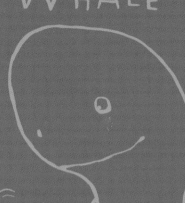

RAT

ROACH

MOOSE

CHILD

BOAR

VIKING
Published by Penguin Group
Penguin Young Readers Group, 345 Hudson Street, New York, New York 10014, U.S.A.
Penguin Group (Canada), 90 Eglinton Avenue East, Suite 700, Toronto, Ontario, Canada M4P 2Y3
(a division of Pearson Penguin Canada Inc.)
Penguin Books Ltd, 80 Strand, London WC2R 0RL, England
Penguin Ireland, 25 St Stephen's Green, Dublin 2, Ireland (a division of Penguin Books Ltd)
Penguin Group (Australia), 250 Camberwell Road, Camberwell, Victoria 3124, Australia
(a division of Pearson Australia Group Pty Ltd)
Penguin Books India Pvt Ltd, 11 Community Centre, Panchsheel Park, New Delhi – 110 017, India
Penguin Group (NZ), Cnr Airborne and Rosedale Roads, Albany, Auckland 1310, New Zealand
(a division of Pearson New Zealand Ltd)
Penguin Books (South Africa) (Pty) Ltd, 24 Sturdee Avenue, Rosebank, Johannesburg 2196, South Africa

Penguin Books Ltd, Registered Offices: 80 Strand, London WC2R 0RL, England

First published in 2003 in Germany by Peter Hammer Verlag
First published in the United States of America in 2006 by Viking, a division of Penguin Young Readers Group

10 9 8 7 6 5 4 3 2 1

Illustrations copyright © Nadia Budde, 2003
Text copyright © Jeremy Fitzkee, 2003
LIBRARY OF CONGRESS CATALOGING-IN-PUBLICATION DATA
Fitzkee, Jeremy.
One, two, three, me / by Jeremy Fitzkee ; illustrations by Nadia Budde.
p. cm.
Summary: Unexpected rhymes such as half/giraffe and towel/owl show the silly sounds of everyday words.
ISBN 0-670-06124-7 (hardcover)
[1. Rhyme—Fiction. 2. Stories in rhyme.] I. Budde, Nadia, ill. II. Title.
PZ8.3.F635723One 2006
[E]—dc22
2005023320

Manufactured in China

ONE

THREE

TWO

ME

NADIA BUDDE
JEREMY FITZKEE

VIKING

SUE   MOLLY   CLAIRE   POLAR BEAR

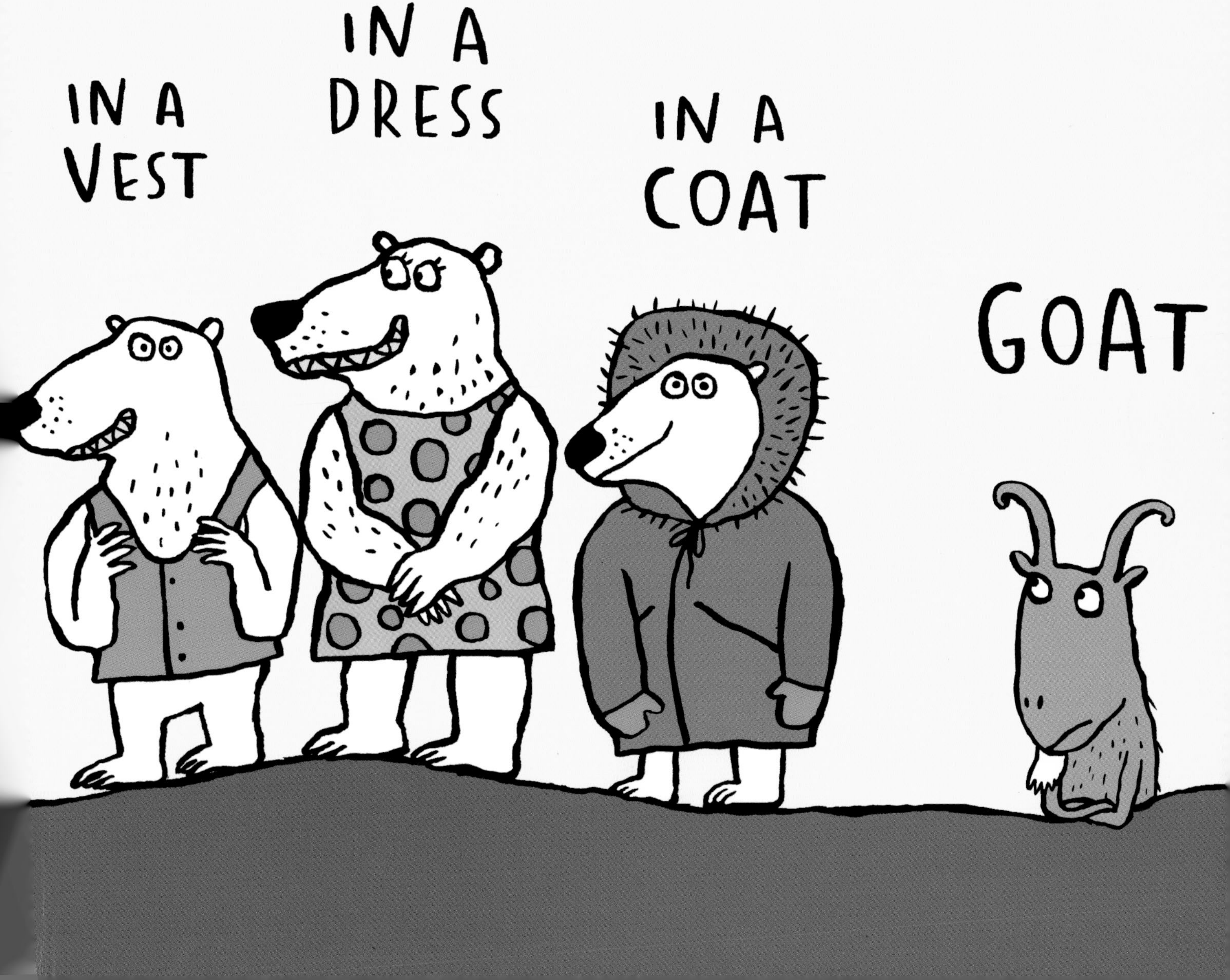
IN A VEST
IN A DRESS
IN A COAT
GOAT

IN THE
RAIN

IN THE
SNOW

IN THE
FOG

FROG

BLONDE

BRUNETTE

HALF
AND
HALF

GIRAFFE

WITH A NECKLACE

WITH A FEATHER

WITH A BROOCH

ROACH

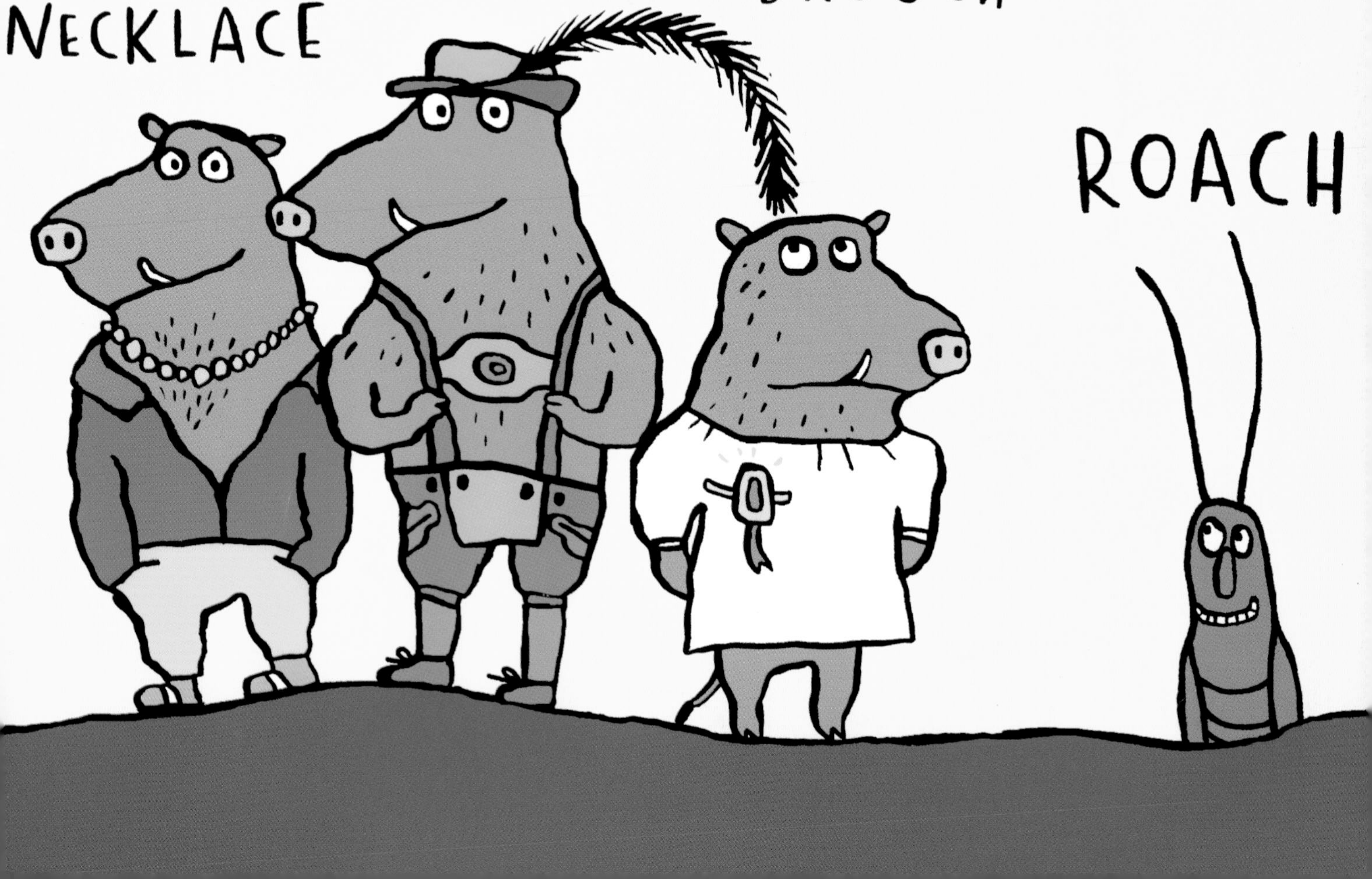

SHY TAME WILD CHILD

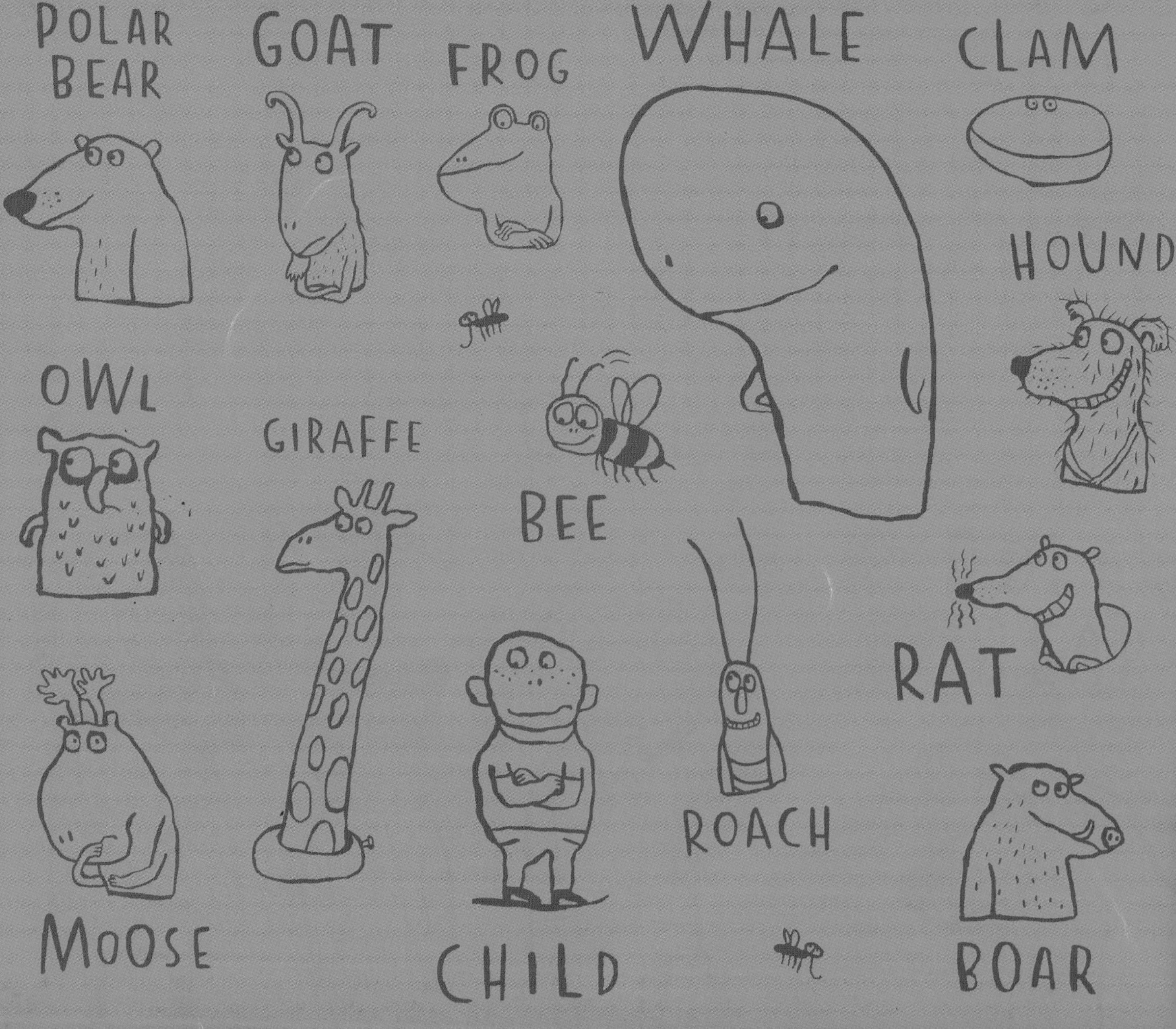

POLAR BEAR

GOAT

FROG

WHALE

CLAM

HOUND

OWL

GIRAFFE

BEE

OWL

RAT

MOOSE

GIRAFFE

CHILD

ROACH

BOAR